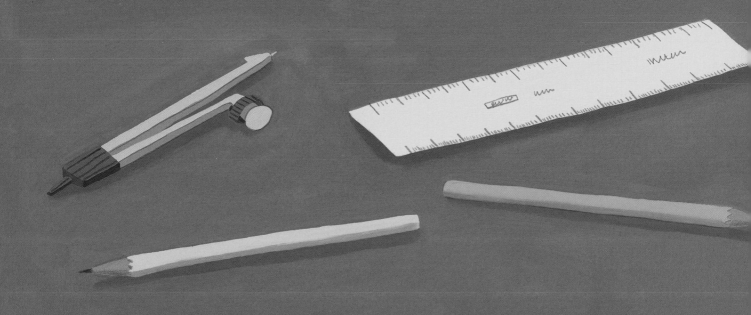

Kathryn White has written over a dozen children's books. When she is not writing, Kathryn visits schools and libraries telling stories and leading activities. She lives in England with her husband and children.

Miriam Latimer studied illustration at the University of the West of England. She now works as a full-time illustrator and combines this with workshops for primary school children. Miriam lives with her husband in England. *Ruby's School Walk* is her fifth project with Barefoot Books.

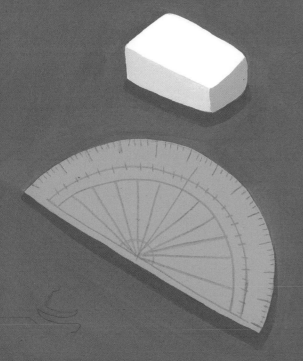

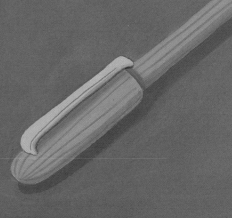

Ruby's School Walk

Barefoot Books
Celebrating Art and Story

For Emily, for making sure I kept Ruby on the path — K. W.
To Pete, Sarah and Rob for your invaluable contribution xx — M. L.

Barefoot Books
2067 Massachusetts Ave
Cambridge, MA 02140

First published in the United States of America in 2010 by Barefoot Books Inc

This book has been printed and bound in China
on 100% acid-free paper by Printplus Ltd

Graphic Design by Beck Ward Murphy
Color reproduction by B & P International, Hong Kong

This book was typeset in Triplex and Hoagie Infant
The illustrations were prepared in acrylic paints and watercolor pencils

ISBN 978-1-84686-275-5

Library of Congress cataloging-in-publication data is available
under LCCN 2009016218

1 3 5 7 9 8 6 4 2

Ruby's School Walk

Written by **Kathryn White**
Illustrated by **Miriam Latimer**

Barefoot Books
Celebrating Art and Story

On the way to school
there's a rushing river.
It's full of **crocodiles**.

Mom says, "It's just the stream,
with silver fish and frogs and logs."

But she's wrong.
I must be brave, I must be strong.

Those crocodiles may
be out of sight, but
they're ready to
snap, **roar** and **bite**.

I've seen their long tails
swirl around

Between the reeds,
without a sound.

So I dance on the bank
in the morning sun,

And my **giant** shadow
makes them run.

On my way to school there's a **haunted** house. It's full of ghosts.

Mom smiles. She says,
"It's just an empty place for sale."
But she's wrong.
I must be brave, I must be strong.

I've seen dark shadows float about,
And **bats** with red eyes peering out,
And **witches** flit around the rooms,
And outside, I've seen witches' brooms.

So I sing my special magic song,
And do my magic **hop-a-long**.

On my way to school there's a **tiger** hiding behind a wall.
Mom smiles.

She says, "That's just
Old Fletcher's tabby cat."
But she's wrong.
I must be brave, I must be strong.

I've seen it open up its jaws
And bare its fangs and jagged claws.
I've seen it **crouch**
                    and **sneak**
                              and **prowl**.

So I bark my loudest, like a hound,
And **growl** and leap and jump
                    and **bound**.

On my way to school
There's a forest
deep and **dark**.

Mom smiles. She says,
"It's just the trees in the park."

But she's wrong.
I must be brave, I must be strong.

The forest's full of **mighty beasts**.
They're hunting around for tasty feasts.
They **loom**, they **lurk** behind the trees,
And call each other on the breeze.

So I shout, "Look out, beasts!
Keep well back!
I've brought my sword,
So don't attack."

At my school, I'm not so sure.
Mom walks with me through the door.
My heart beats fast, my feet go slow.
Mom hangs my bag and turns to go.

I wonder what I'll do today.
I don't know what to think or say.

Mom smiles. She says,
"Ruby, perhaps today you will be
Finding **treasure** in the sea;

Catching **dragons** in the sky,
And teaching **fairies** how to fly;

You'll be teaching
trolls to read and write,
and painting **stars**
to make them bright;

You'll be sailing **ShipS** across the sea,

and setting helpless **mermaids** free."

I hug her so;
I know she's right.

I say, "Bye, Mom,
See you tonight!"

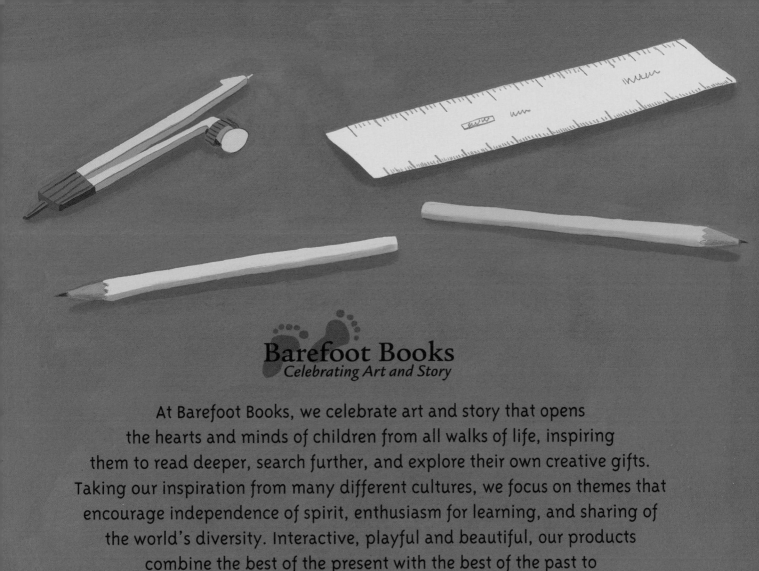

Barefoot Books
Celebrating Art and Story

At Barefoot Books, we celebrate art and story that opens
the hearts and minds of children from all walks of life, inspiring
them to read deeper, search further, and explore their own creative gifts.
Taking our inspiration from many different cultures, we focus on themes that
encourage independence of spirit, enthusiasm for learning, and sharing of
the world's diversity. Interactive, playful and beautiful, our products
combine the best of the present with the best of the past to
educate our children as the caretakers of tomorrow.

Live Barefoot!
Join us at **www.barefootbooks.com**

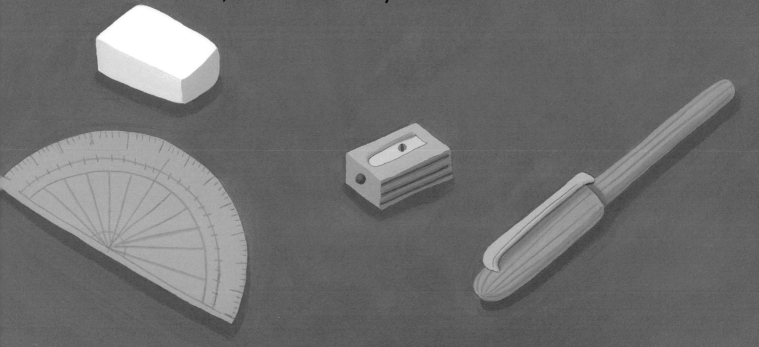